The Gingerbread Boy

Retold by Michèle Dufresne • Illustrated by Tracy La Rue Hohn

PIONEER VALLEY EDUCATIONAL PRESS, INC.

"Look," said the old woman.
"Look at the Gingerbread Boy."

2

"Yum, yum," said the old man.

"You can't catch me,"
said the Gingerbread Boy.

"We can catch you,"
said the old woman.

"We can catch you,"
said the old man.

5

"Look," said the cow.
"Look at the Gingerbread Boy."

6

"Yum, yum," said the horse.

"You can't catch me,"
said the Gingerbread Boy.

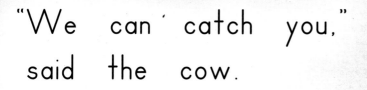

"We can catch you,"
said the cow.

"We can catch you,"
said the horse.

"Oh, no,"
said the Gingerbread Boy.
"Oh, no! Here is a river!"

"Come on," said the fox.
"Come on!"

"Come on," said the fox.
"Come on!"

"Yum, yum," said the fox.